Tales from the

Black

Meadow

Chris Lambert
With illustrations by Nigel Wilson

First published in Great Britain in 2013 by Exiled Publishing, South Street Arts Centre, 21 South Street, Reading, RG1 4QU

Copyright © Chris Lambert July 2013
Illustrations Copyright ©Nigel Wilson July 2013
The moral right of the author has been asserted
All rights reserved

A CIP catalogue record for this book is available from the British Library

ISBN-13: 978-1484171738
ISBN-10: 148417173X

lambertthewriter.blogspot.co.uk
exiledpublications.blogspot.co.uk
soullesscentral.blogspot.com

For Roger Mullins and all those others
lost in the mists.

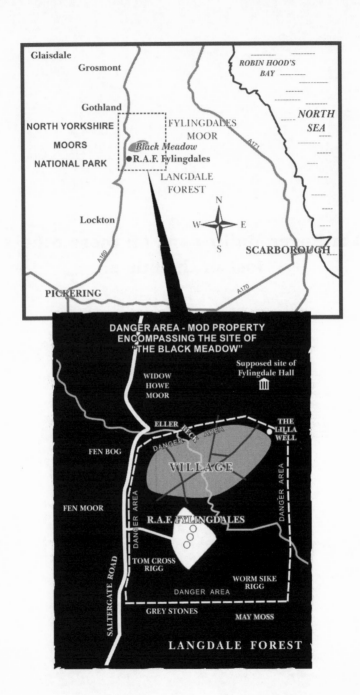

DANGER AREA - MOD PROPERTY
ENCOMPASSING THE SITE OF
"THE BLACK MEADOW"

4

Contents

List of Illustrations

When the mist spreads   74
Like an unspooling ball of wool
Threading over the land

And it was this gentleman that the Devil decided to meet one   76
Saturday evening.

He was shocked to see that where the dwellings of workers   84
once stood that young trees burst through the shattered
rooftops.

His choice of subject remained the same; the standing stone   94
in the centre of the meadow.

The old woman stood outside, behind the gate, looking at   102
the house.

... in the distance, by the well, he saw a figure with   124
black oil dripping skin ...

He looked up from where he lay and saw at the window   132
the dark black head with its shining eyes glaring in.

Roger Mullins
On the borders of the Black Meadow
(North Yorkshire Moors – Near RAF Fylingdales)
October 14th 1969

Photograph reprinted with the permission of Professor Philip Hull – University of York

Introduction

When Professor R. Mullins of the University of York went missing in 1972 in an area of North Yorkshire known as Black Meadow, he left behind an extensive body of work that provided a great insight into the folklore of this mysterious place.

Mullins, a classics professor, had a great interest in Black Meadow folklore and spent many years documenting the tales that were part of the local oral tradition.

In his office, his colleagues found over twenty thick notebooks crammed with stories and interviews from the villages around Black Meadow. Some of these stories seemed to be from the legendary disappearing village itself and provided some vital clues as to how the phenomena was interpreted and explained by the local populace.

These stories, poems and songs have been gathered together to capture the unsettling nature of the Black Meadow.

Do not read this on your own at night and make sure you shut your windows. Listen for the stamping feet of the horsemen, avoid the gaze of the Watcher in the village and do not walk into the mist.

Chris Lambert

Can you tell me if or where I shall see my child again?

Can you tell me maiden fair?

Can you tell me, maiden fair
Can you tell me if or where
I shall see my child again
Walk upon the fields of men?
Will she ever stumble back
From the meadow all a'black?
Will she sit upon her chair?
Will I hear her on the stair?
Tell me now, my spirits fall
I cannot hear my daughter call.

(Traditional)

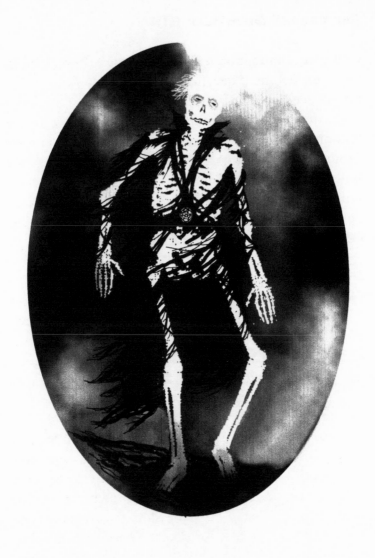

It is said there is a man who looks as though he is made of rag and bone.

The Rag and Bone Man

It is said there is a man who looks as though he is made of rag and bone.

It is said that he is seven feet tall, thin and brittle as a dry old stick, with a face so thin that his grey skin looks as though it is stretched over the skull of a giant rat. He wears a dark coat that trails down to the floor wrapped around his skeletal frame. The coat is held closed by a ruby clasp which never opens unless he is given cause to scream.

Some say he was once a handsome farmer who owned thirty acres at the centre of Black Meadow. He grew grain and kept cows and sheep. He had a beautiful wife and six darling children. He was happy, they were happy, even the cows and sheep were happy.

That all changed when one day the local squire visited the farm. The Squire coveted the land and the farmer's wife. He offered to buy it and her for a meagre price. When the farmer refused, the squire ordered four of his strongest men to take the children to the carriage outside. The farmer tried to stop them, but the four men battered him down, beat his skull with stones from the old wall until it was thin, brittle, elongated and misshapen like the skull of a rat. They tied his feet to the old iron boot-scraper that was bolted to the doorstep and his hands to the carriage. With his children's screams ringing in his ears, they commanded the horses to charge away. And all the time the farmer could hear his lovely wife, inside his house, begging the squire to stop. When the farmer was quiet and stretched and the children were quietly sobbing, the squire dragged the farmer's wife out of the bedroom whilst his men set fire to the house. The four men threw the battered body into the burning building. All that was found were the rags and bones of the poor farmer.

On the ruins of the farm it is said that the squire built a beautiful village, charged rent for the lovely houses and became extremely rich. It is said that in his mansion was a silent maid who cried whilst she scrubbed the flagstones. It is said that he made a small fortune selling six darling children into servitude.

But the villagers were not happy. They started happy but did not stay that way. One day, ten years after the village was built, the children were playing in the field when at the end of the lane there appeared a tall figure, thin like an old dry stick, clad in a long black cloak with a ruby clasp. The children had been laughing, school had finished and summer had arrived. But then they heard the scream, the horrible scream of the Rag and Bone man.

The Rag and Bone Man has a long coat that he only opens when he screams. He only screams when the villagers are happy or when the children are laughing. It is said that within his scream can be heard the crackling of flames, six children crying in terror, a wife being violated and the mutilation of a loving husband. And when he opens his coat, smoke and fog billow out, swallowing the village whole.

But he is thin and brittle like a dry old stick so he cannot hold the village forever. Now and again he opens his coat, causing its return. When the mist rises the village comes. But no matter how pretty it looks, if the people of the village smile or the children laugh, if you are there, if you walk through that village, you too will hear the cry of the Rag and Bone Man and if you do, we shall not see you again.

*He rose up and put his feet together. His toes stretched,
bursting out of his worn out shoes and dug themselves into the
ground. He thrust his arms above his head, screaming as they
stretched and split into branches.*

The Shining Apples

Once upon a time there was a young girl. She had bright green eyes and golden hair that grew down past her knees. Her feet were bare and she had no hat upon her head. No one knew her name or where she came from, but one sunny August day she walked into a village just on the outskirts of the Black Meadow.

She was skinny and wore a tatty cotton dress. On her arm was a large basket filled with shining yellow apples. Each one was perfectly round and unbruised. She called out in a small shrill voice if anyone would like to buy her shining apples. Some children came running; they saw how delicious the apples looked and asked how much they cost. She said that she would give all the apples away for a pair of shoes and a hat. The children ran home. One found an old pair of shoes he didn't want, whilst another found a straw hat that had belonged to his grandmother before she died. As they returned they saw that the local vagabond was walking towards her. He pushed the little girl to the floor and snatched her basket. The vagabond ran away, sat at the side of the road, eating the apples; cores and all.

The children helped the little girl with long golden hair to her feet. They were so sorry for her that they gave her the hat and shoes without asking for anything in return. The girl thanked them for their kindness, wiping the tears from her face. She said that for their kindness they could have all the apples that they ever desired, whenever they needed them.

She put on the shoes, placed the hat upon her head and walked towards the vagabond who was sat by the side of the road, scoffing his third apple, core and all. The vagabond looked up at the little girl. She pointed a finger at him, a tear dripped from the end of her finger onto the apple he was holding in his hand. He laughed at her cruelly and bit into the apple. As all the children watched, the vagabond appeared to stiffen, his skin cracked and darkened until it looked like wood. He rose up and put his feet together. His toes stretched, bursting out of his worn out shoes and dug themselves into the ground. He thrust his arms above his head, screaming as they stretched and split into branches. Leaves appeared from the top of his head. His clothes transformed into bark, growing and enveloping him, until what was once a man was now a tree. The many new branches sprouted blossom. The blossom fell. Tiny buds appeared growing into shining apples.

The little girl picked up the basket, walked a short way and left the road before disappearing into the depths of the Black Meadow. No one ever saw her again. The villagers stripped the tree of its beautiful fruit, mixing them into delicious jams and ciders, the like of which had never been tasted before.

The next morning the tree had vanished, but several years later in a village 15 miles away, it was reported that a tree had suddenly appeared that bore the most incredible apples. And it is still said, that even now when a village is hungry, a tree will appear on the outskirts of the Black Meadow, a tree with shining yellow apples.

... and they danced now these Horsemen, they danced and danced wildly; their faces joyous and their eyes bright and full of life ...

The Horsemen

If October is warm in the Black Meadow then the Horsemen will dance.

It was late October. Everything about the year had been late; the harvest only just brought in, the spring in summer and the summer in autumn – resulting in a balmy October. November was near. Shirtless farmhands still toiled in the dirt, maidens walked without scarves, still wearing sunny cotton caps upon their heads.

The horses whinnied and snorted in their stuffy stables. They stamped their feet, filling the night with frenzied neighs to be free, to let a breeze cool their hides.

And where the people should have all been gathered inside, drinking warm mulled cider or eating grandmamma's apple pie, they eschewed this in favour of ale and water on the steps of their houses. They sang songs into the dark while the horses stamped their feet, snorting to be let out, to let the October night excite their nostrils.

And the people would say that if a third night of warmth occurred in October without interruption, the Horsemen would come and the Horsemen would dance. It was said that no one should witness this, it was secret. It was for the Horsemen alone. It was not for human eyes.

But, as is the way in such stories, there was a little boy who was far too curious for his own good. He was eight years old and had never experienced a warm October in his life. Indeed the last one had occurred thirty-five years previously.

The third night came. The young boy had been told to stay inside, but he was always curious. He had spied the local vagrant stealing eggs, listened to the argument between the butcher and his wife. He had even seen the vicar kissing the milkmaid on the nose.

His mother had tucked him into bed, just under a single sheet, as the night was so close. She shut the door. Once the boy could hear his mother shouting at his father again he opened the window to climb down the drainpipe.

His father had told him that the horsemen gathered in the grazing meadow and that to watch them meant oblivion.

But, as is the way in these stories, the boy would not listen to his father. The boy would not be sensible or good so, on this the third night of the first warm October in thirty-five years, a young boy who ignored old tales and disobeyed the advice of his elders, climbed out of his bedroom window before walking towards the grazing meadow.

As he passed the stable he stopped, for the noise of the horses was most distracting. The incessant whinnying and the stamping hooves broke through the quiet night.

As the boy walked closer to the stables, he saw, to his surprise, the chief groom of the village unbolting the stable doors and pulling them slowly open. The horses leapt out, pushing the door back in their eagerness and knocking the smiling groom to the floor. They galloped towards the grazing meadow. The groom staggered to his feet waving, grinning and shouting, "Dance! Dance!"

The boy crept towards the grazing meadow, where he saw that the horses had slowed to a trot before coming to a stop. In fact, they stood silent, staring, as though waiting. From the village came a series of sounds; windows and doors banging open, sounds of excitement, clapping and shrieking. Slowly the sound died away. Initially there was dead silence. The horses stood still, they hardly seemed to breathe, they did not snort, their tails didn't flick, and their ears didn't flutter.

From the village there came a low sound. A solid thump, thump, thump on a marching drum. The boy thought that this could be the drum that belonged to the Mayor's nephew, who always led the village band in the carnival parade at Easter. It was soon joined by the church bell ringing, ringing, ringing in time with the thump, thump, thump.

Still the horses didn't move.

Three guitars started strumming from the windows of different houses. One would have been indistinct but three were quite clear. The church organ joined the sound, the drone escaping through the entrance left open by the milkmaid-kissing priest. All of this was clear but not loud. Other instruments joined the fray; piano keys leaked through open windows, penny whistles and flutes were playing from yards, whilst the barman's harmonium added a sweep and volume.

And still the horses didn't move.

The voices began. The first was deep and sonorous. The second voice was light and warming. His mother and father were singing. Other voices joined theirs. The village was alive with sound.

And the horses began to move.

They stomped their feet to the rhythm, fluttered their ears and swished their tails. As the beat increased in tempo, so too did the speed of the horses stamping. They began to move into a circle, stepping in and out, in and out. The voices raised in volume. The tempo increased. Faster and faster and faster. The horses jumped higher, galloping to and fro, swapping places across the circle, getting faster but always dancing in time to the swelling music.

Suddenly the horses began to rear up on to their hind legs, but rather than stamp back onto all fours they remained, dancing upright.

The boy blinked his disbelieving eyes, the unlikely sight, which, as is the way in these stories, became more unlikely the more he stared. The horses stretched their legs. Their bodies seemed to thin and shrink. Their long faces shortened. Their manes became shocks of messy hair upon their suddenly round human heads. Their tails were pulled inside their behinds. Their ears no longer fluttered, but slipped from the tops to the sides of their heads. Their hind hooves flattened, softened and grew toes. Their dark hides faded, becoming pale skin. And they danced now, these *Horsemen*. They danced and danced wildly, their faces joyous and their eyes bright and full of life.

The boy watched, mesmerised at the change. He marvelled at the enchanting noise sweeping out of the village into his ears. His limbs shook and his feet stamped. He rose to his feet, running into the field where the Horsemen danced. When they saw him they smiled and patted his back. They taught him steps of such skill, that were he ever to woo a young lady with this new dance, he would be guaranteed a quick wedding and many children.

And he danced and danced. The night grew old.

The music slowed. The voices dimmed. The boy found himself stopping with the rest of the Horsemen. The organ faded. The bell no longer tolled. The guitars stopped their strumming. Finally the thump, thump, thump of the marching drum ceased.

Standing still in the field were the horses, plus one new foal.

Of course you will know of the shriek from the boy's mother when she found his bed disturbed and him gone. You will know of the cry of the father when he saw the new foal asleep in the stable. The new foal grew to be a splendid stallion that was always given the finest hay. The mother prayed for another warm October but there were no more in her lifetime.

The next warm October occurred fifty years later. The boy's mother and father had been dead for over three decades. On the third night the groom opened the stables. The villagers brought out the instruments to play for the Horsemen.

Halfway through the dance an old man walked out of the field. He trudged towards an empty house. The villagers stopped the music and stared.

They whispered to one another. They pointed and shook their heads in wonder. A child had disappeared from that very house, on a balmy October night, many years ago.

In Her Arms of Mist

I can't see my hand
In front of my face
Can't walk another step
This place so dark
But I knock so hard
And the door becomes
Your room your face

You don't wait you want
To take my hand
And pull me to your side
Your mouth so soft
It's not quite there
And I can't see
I know you're there

Wake so quick
The ground so hard
My arms are scratched
The room so dark
The breeze blows hard
About my head
I did not hear
What she had said

So close and yet so cold

*(Discovered scratched in the oak panel of a tavern bench by Roger
Mullins in 1965)*

Our Fair Land (A song)

Mist and Heather call us soft
Over bramble meadows
Village field and apple loft
Under land and hedgerows

> *Will you not hear the call?*
> *Will you with us stand?*
> *Will you take our hands in yours?*
> *Wake our fairest land.*

Church bell rings out, strong and proud
Horse hooves tramp in sweet time
Voices, drums that play so loud
Trap their dance in sweet rhyme

> *Will you not hear the call?*
> *Will you with us stand?*
> *Will you take our hands in yours?*
> *Wake our fairest land.*

Hidden cave and darkened sphere
Rag and bone and scream
Shining apples hold no fear
For this waking dream

> *Will you not hear the call?*
> *Will you with us stand?*
> *Will you take our hands in yours?*
> *Wake our fairest land.*

(Traditional)

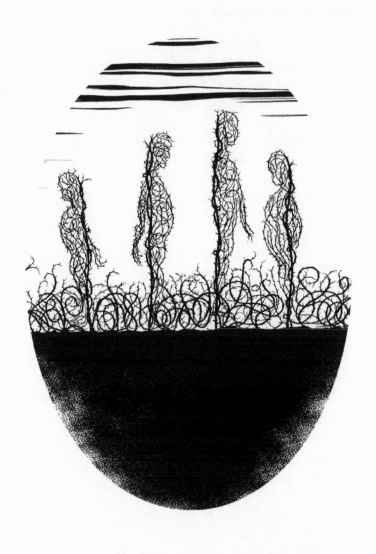

The brambles started to grow in thick clumps on the pillars, long straight clumps at each side, two little clumps at the base and a round clump on the top.

The Children of the Black Meadow

It has long been said that the Black Meadow has a mystical power. There are so many tales and songs that if put together they would fill the shelves of Saltburn library. Some of these tales offer comfort, others horror and some an answer to the mysteries of the Black Meadow. Some of the tales do all three of these things.

The land has a sacred relationship with those who toil upon it and those who live by it. The land seems to give something back to those that gave it life.

There was a time when sheep, cows and horses could not graze upon the Black Meadow as the ground was covered in tangles of blackberry. Only the bravest, clad in their strongest boots and toughest leather trousers, or the most desperate, could walk into the field.

Once there was a beautiful family who lived on the edge of the blackberry meadow. The four children, each born a year apart, lived a jolly and gay existence. They picked the blackberries in the late summer, braving the brambles, making dens and mazes in the knotted tangles of thorny branches.

One heart-breaking night in April, the house caught alight while the four children lay asleep. Their mother and father beat at the door. They battled the flames but all that was found in the morning were four sets of blackened bones.

The village mourned the loss of these sweet and laughing children. The mother visited the graveside every day, while the father grew despondent, spending his evenings at the tavern. The two never spoke to one another again in public. Most suspected it was the same behind closed doors. Four months later another tragedy struck. Whilst stumbling home from the tavern, the father tripped, hitting his head on the bottom step outside his front door. He died instantly.

The mother stood silent at the grave days later, her face stoic and unmoving. As the months passed she sat in her house by the window only venturing out for goods and the occasional book, for it seemed that she had become a voracious reader. The books she read were reported to be somewhat esoteric in nature, but no one ever asked her to explain why she was reading such mysterious works.

Over the space of a week, there were several peculiar happenings that occurred one after the other. Firstly the graves of the children were disturbed and, on closer examination, it became clear that the bones had been removed. Secondly, it was noticed on her weekly visit to the village shop, that the mother had hundreds of tiny cuts on her arms and hands as though from many tiny thorns. The final and most disturbing of these happenings was that this same, poor, sad mother of four dead children was seen late at night on the edge of the blackberry meadow lighting fires around the perimeter; six fires at six points, like the six points of a star.

No one questioned the mother about this; she barely spoke to anyone, although some people heard her talking on the edge of the meadow. Some thought that they heard her calling the children she had lost by name, calling them in from play.

Weeks passed into months. The mother stood looking out over the meadow every morning as though expecting something or someone to appear. It was at the end of the third month of this that a single bramble shoot was sighted above all the others standing straight and tall like a beanpole above the tangled mess below. Over the succeeding weeks another appeared, followed by two more, each one appearing a week apart, standing clear against the horizon.

From all around each stalk, other brambles began to climb up, adding form and body to the thick blackberry spine in the centre. The brambles grew around each stalk until they were each the shape of a pillar. Four pillars stood atop of the tangle of brambles below, like standing stones on a forgotten hill. The pillars of brambles changed even more over the following weeks. The brambles started to grow in thick clumps on the pillars, long straight clumps at each side, two little clumps at the base and a round clump on the top. These clumps grew more distinct in their shape until, one by one each resembled a person cut by a skilled topiarist.

The next week people were surprised to notice that the first pillar to appear had gone. In the weeks that followed the others too all vanished. It was then that the villagers noticed something far more shocking and out of place. The mother was smiling.

The villagers finally understood what had happened several months later. There had been rumours of course, people had noticed lanterns flickering at the children's bedroom windows. They had seen the woman hanging torn washing with a serene smile on her face, but that was nothing compared to the day she returned to the church.

It was the Sunday before Easter. The church was packed with villagers listening to the sermon. Suddenly the priest was struck into silence, his face becoming pale as he looked up the aisle to the doors. There, silhouetted in the sunlight was the mother with four figures clad in her children's torn Sunday best. The two smaller figures, standing either side of her, were holding her scratched, bleeding hands in their tight and nervous bramble grip. She walked forward, grinning. They sat in the pew that she and her family had occupied so many Sundays previously. Now she sat with her bramble children with their tangled arms and thorny legs; these creatures made of twisted thorn and leaf. People tried not to stare but these children invited it, looking around, their blackberry eyes unblinking in the stained glass light. The mother smiled. She nodded at the priest who continued his sermon - which no-one listened to - in a shaking voice.

The following days grew even stranger, for the children returned to school holding their books and satchels in their prickly hands. They sat silent in class, but then so did the other children, terrified as they were of those silent unblinking blackberry eyes. Some of the pupils were brave enough to follow them home. They reported that when the four children went inside, they could be seen, each standing in a large earth-filled pot, whilst their mother poured water over them.

The villagers noticed how quiet the mother was becoming. They had seen her kissing her children farewell at the school gate, her face cut by their bramble lips, but her initial euphoria had passed. She seemed quieter and thoughtful.

Another grave was disturbed.

The mother was seen at the edge of the meadow again, with her fires and incantations. Over the coming weeks and months, people witnessed the thickest and strongest bramble they had ever seen,

There, silhouetted in the sunlight was the mother and four figures clad in her children's torn Sunday best ...

rising above the rest with other brambles wrapping around it to make a sturdy pillar.

Everybody kept checking the growth of the bramble every day; they were determined to see the magic done. Finally, after several weeks, a giant bramble man stood above the tangle. As they watched from behind their twitching curtains and half opened doors, they saw this giant bramble man stroll across the top of the blackberry to the woman he loved, enfolding her in his prickly embrace. She wept. He stared unblinking from his blackberry eyes.

As the weeks passed and the children of the village gave the blackberry four a wide berth, things seemed to go less well for the mother. Villagers could hear her shouting and doors slamming, they could only hear her voice as the bramble father had none. The bramble father was seen every night sitting in a corner of the tavern pouring beer into his bramble mouth, watching as it dripped over the thorns inside him before making a puddle on the floor. No one sat with him. One night the bramble father smashed his glass on the floor in a rage and stood, knocking his stool aside. He walked outside towards the field. Looking down at his bramble chest, he saw a small branch curling out from between his thorny ribs. He pulled it with both hands, tying the trailing bramble to a post outside the tavern. He walked slowly towards the field, gradually unravelling as he trudged further away from the village. He walked, with his slowly disappearing bramble head held high, until all that was left was a single trail of bramble running from the tavern, across the street and deep into the heart of the blackberry meadow.

The next morning more doors slammed. The mother screamed for them to stay, but the children wanted to return to their father. The village hated and feared them. They could not bear it a moment longer. The mother argued, pleading with them not to untangle, not to join the blackberry as their father had. Her tears were such that they relented, but they would not stay. The next morning the four blackberry children donned ripped caps and shredded clothes. With their mother's sobs echoing in their tangled ears, they went to seek their fortune in the south of the country where, it is said, that they made thousands of pounds in the manufacturing, marketing and selling of the most delicious cordial.

Novo Inventus

What will you find when you pull back the bramble?

A forgotten coin
An old book of rhymes
A roast dinner still steaming on a plate
A tub of golden apples
The bloodied claw of a buzzard
A screaming child

What will come out of the mist?

Four children of bramble
A vagabond tree
A horned demon
Three spheres of dark
A spiral spinning home

(Found in a child's exercise book on the ruined site of Black Meadow School)

There is a standing stone in the centre of Black Meadow.

The Standing Stone

There is a standing stone in the centre of Black Meadow.

It is a rough oblong of black-grey granite with ornate carvings up the sides. Each carving is a different sized spiral scattered all over the uneven seven sides of the eleven-foot-tall pillar.

The standing stone is in the centre of a treacherous bog. To some it is impassable; to others it seems hardly worth the bother, after all it is just a large lump of granite. Some have lost their lives and many have lost their shoes there.

People who think that it is not worth the effort ought to read up on their local folklore. If they did they would see that a visit to the standing stone might be a worthwhile venture.

It has been said that when a gentleman or lady visits the stone they will need to take with them a large sheet of parchment and a stick of charcoal or dark wax. It is advised that a visitor to the stone scrutinises every inch until they find their spiral. Apparently, legend states, that the visitor will know that spiral when they see it. The spiral will stand out as though embossed and shining, rather than engraved and dull. If two were to visit the stone each of them would see a different spiral and will comment or even argue that a different spiral is standing out.

It is said that one should place the parchment over the chosen spiral and rub the wax or charcoal over the pattern until it is captured on the paper.

Once the individual has negotiated the treacherous bog home, they should take the parchment and lay it flat on a table. It has been noted that there is a space between the lines of the spiral in which one could write using tiny characters. The individual may have something or, heaven forbid someone, that they would like to vanish. They can use the spiral to enable such a thing to occur.

Some examples of items that individuals have vanished include:
A lustful thought
A painful memory
An annoying barking hound belonging to a neighbour
A disease on your lung
An unrelenting ache of the knee
An unsightly wart
A nagging spouse
An irritating younger brother

It is suggested that one should write down (neatly and with joined handwriting) the name or description of this item within the spiral and where it shall be at the midnight of that day. It must be written clearly so that another can read it. If someone has an untidy scrawl, then caution must be exercised, in case that person should lose the wrong thing, such as a whole memory, a nose, a home or an entire village.

It is said that this paper should be thrown upon a fire and that the individual should watch the ash and smoke spiral up the chimney.

It is said that the spiral of ash and smoke will find the offending item that has been identified and grow or shrink to envelop it, until it, he or she is hidden. The spiral of ash and smoke will dance back to the stone where it will deposit its luggage inside.

With this simple process one can be free of a burden whilst a standing stone in the centre of Black Meadow will become ever so slightly larger.

(Adapted from Recorded Conversations with a Meadow Witch *by R. Mullins- Notes III)*

On the same day a labourer reported a strange feeling as though someone was with him in the plough shed. Over the following days the vicar felt spied upon through the vestry window, the milkmaid felt watched in the meadow, the butcher's child in the heather, a skipping girl in her own yard ...

The Watcher from the Village

Who was the watcher in the village?

For as long as everyone could remember, people felt as though they were being watched by someone or something. This had been going on for generations. It went back to a story that grandchildren told their grandchildren and those grandchildren had told theirs.

In the centre of the village was a well. No one was sure how deep it was or how long ago it had been dug. It had always been there, some said that the village had been built around it. The bucket for the well had a tremendously long rope attached because, in times of drought, the water was so far down that a pebble would make its splash in the time it would take the Old Soak to walk from his house to the tavern. Yet at night the people would talk of the Watcher from the well, a dark figure who would rise from the depths and stand in the centre of the village, turning his head slowly from side to side until sunrise. During a drought, on a sunny day, an opening could be seen far down in the side of the shaft; an opening large enough for an animal or man to crawl through. Was this where the Watcher came from?

An adventurous youth, one dry summer, was lowered down to the opening with a lantern. He reported that this opening was actually a tunnel that stretched on into the black. The boy wanted to come back up, but was given promise of fine cake and ale if he would dare crawl down and return with news of what lay at the very end. Reluctantly the youth agreed, squeezing himself into the hole while his friends above watched the light of his lantern fade from sight.

They waited for an incredibly long time. Some said it was an hour and a half, while others said it was closer to three. They began to fear what may have happened to their brave friend. They tried to fathom what excuse they would have to make to his terrifying mother for his disappearance. As the shadows began to grow long, they braced themselves to go to the family home and bear the terrible tidings. Suddenly, they heard a shout. Turning to see where it had come from, they saw, walking up the street, their muddy friend. His clothes were torn, his hair covered in leaves and bits of bramble.

The brave youth told them that he had crawled in a straight line for hundreds of yards, finding that the tunnel sloped steadily upwards until, after a good hour of crawling, he had found himself in the centre of the blackberry field.

So was there a Watcher at the bottom of the well? Was that same watcher from the blackberry field? The youth had put a marker down where he had made his exit and the friends all went to look at the hole from which he had made his escape. Upon examination, they realised that the entrance and the beginning of the slope had been paved by someone, centuries ago, judging by the mossy and lichen-ridden appearance. Perhaps it was the same age as the well itself?

The news of this discovery, which spread like wildfire, did nothing to curb the feeling of being watched. Now it was being rumoured that the black robed figure could be seen not only in the centre of the village but also from within the field of Blackberry looking out at the villagers. This feeling, this fear of being watched, grew and grew to such intensity that they feared to leave their own homes, even though nothing tangible had even been witnessed or seen, only rumoured. People were jumping at shadows.

The seeds of this terror began with the Old Soak who few listened to and fewer ever believed, but in this time of suspicion even *his* wild tales began to gain credence. When he said he saw something in the blackberry this started a storm of rumours and frightened speculation.

The day after his revelation, the baker's wife swore that she spotted someone at her parlour window. On the same day a labourer reported a strange feeling as though someone was with him in the plough shed. Over the following days the vicar felt spied upon through the vestry window, the milkmaid felt watched in the meadow, the butcher's child in the heather, a skipping girl in her own yard and two or three people swore that someone was definitely in the well.

The priest called a meeting and it was then, that for a moment, things began to calm down.

It is incredible how pleasant one can feel when people begin talking to one another. A great calm descended as neighbour turned to neighbour and shared their nightmarish stories. As they conversed, a reassuring picture began to emerge. It appeared that the Old Soak had made everyone jittery. On the day following his report of something in the blackberry, the adventurous youth had seen a figure float from there to the baker's house. He had bravely followed and looked in at the parlour window. The baker's wife saw, what they now knew was the youth, head towards the plough shed and had sent her husband in pursuit. The baker happened upon the labourer and went back to the house via the church. The labourer, having sensed someone in the plough shed with him, ran outside and saw someone heading for the church. He ran to the vestry and, assuming this figure had gone inside, saw the priest through the window. When he realised his mistake he ran back to the plough shed and was seen by the priest, who had come out of the church, as he passed the meadow. The priest gave chase but stopped, distracted at the sight of the milkmaid resting in the field. Considering that his spying upon the maid might be misconstrued he made his way back to the church, past the heather where the milkmaid, now pursuing him, saw the butcher's child. The butcher's child followed the milkmaid, losing her by the tiler's yard, where he gave up and went to pick blackberries. The tiler's daughter, interrupted in the midst of some energetic skipping saw what she thought was her watcher disappear into the blackberry and bravely made chase. She happened upon the hole leading to the well and, assuming that the mysterious watcher of the village had escaped in there, abandoned all thoughts for her own safety and climbed to the well. The tiler's daughter crawled her way to the end of the tunnel and saw far above her, at the mouth of the well, several figures about to draw water. They appeared startled by the sight of two eyes blinking up at them from the darkness.

The villagers all clapped each other on the back, laughing heartily at their foolishness. What joy abounded at the realisation that it was they who had been watching each other.

They exited the church, skipping towards the tavern under the now darkening sky. Several of the villagers stopped and looked up. Others, wondering what had caught their attention stopped too, until all of the villagers stood, stock-still, looking up in terrified silence into the two enormous eyes that stared back at them from the sky. The villagers didn't move, they barely breathed. The two enormous eyes blinked at them and continued to stare. The villagers abandoned their plans for the tavern, immediately scattered to their various homes, locking the doors behind them and slamming the shutters on every window.

Then, apart from the whites of the two enormous eyes floating above the village, the whole of Black Meadow was plunged into blackness.

Fields of Blackberry

Come out of the mists my friends
Sail the fields of blackberry
Part the fog and wave "Halloo"
Take our hands so tightly
Don't you part and don't you go
When the mists are far away
Come out of the mists my friends
Sail the fields of blackberry

I can see the old flint tower
Your house in the valley
I am counting hour by hour
I know you cannot tarry
But your hair so long and your eyes so clear
And your breath so sweet on my face
Keep out of the mists my friend
Sail the fields of blackberry

The devil has a wicked way
Of keeping lovers parted
But none more than the blackberry mist
That makes me broken hearted
For your love lasts long but I see you not
Though I know that you are so close
Come out of the mist my love
Come and will you tarry?

(Traditional)

The first sphere diverted from its straight line as it passed the church and floated towards the lantern.

The Land Spheres

It is often wondered how Black Meadow got its name. Like so many questions about the area there is always more than one definitive answer. The obvious answer is that it is named after the fields of blackberry that dominate parts of the meadow. Another answer is the Land Spheres.

In 1543 during the winter the first recorded instance of the growing mist occurred. It was said to spread from a central point and expand across the whole meadow. With it came tales of vanishings and a spreading darkness.

There was a great house to the north of the village called Fylingdales Hall. It is now a heath covered pile of rubble. A grand but nervous squire lived there with his wife, four children and extensive household. The Squire's name was Matthew Wilkes and his wife is said to have been called Elizabeth. The children were Jeremiah (7), Edward (6), Mary (5) and Michael (4). There is no record of the names of the servants.

The house could be seen from the village, it stood on a low hill and a well-kept carriageway led up to its impressive oak door. At night-time every window was lit by a candle or a lantern, for the squire was rich and it was thought that he kept a store of candles in an upstairs room. Some say that this was because he greatly feared the dark and battled this terror by putting light wherever there was darkness.

Every night, members of his household would walk along the corridors, winding up and down the stairs, lighting candles in every window. As the night progressed they replaced any that had melted down to the base with a new candle from the store.

So Fylingdales Hall lit the land like a glittering beacon for all to see. It was a beautiful and sparkling sight to behold; tiny glittering lights in every window breaking the blackness with their little yellow spots. Although Matthew Wilkes's fear was laughable to most, none could deny the beauty of the house, especially in the long dark nights of winter. On warm summer nights young lovers would often climb the hill overlooking the house, their embracing silhouettes breaking the pattern of candlelight.

It was on the late afternoon of 15 May that the first recording of the mist appears. The parish records stated that the mist was seen spreading over the bramble field and into the village. Although the mist had been seen before, some spoke of its shocking coldness and of a terrible dark within its centre. The people of the village were afraid but heartened to see that the house could be seen through the fog.

Matthew Wilkes had shut all the windows and doors to ensure that every candle burnt undisturbed. For once people didn't scoff at him. They followed suit lighting every lantern, brazier, fire and candle they could lay their hands on, fighting against that feeling; that strange dark feeling that grew but was intangible.

It was in the evening that things took a turn for the peculiar. People reported a black dot in the mist on the horizon. A few minutes later they reported that the dot appeared to be growing. After several members of the village gathered to look, it was agreed that the dot wasn't growing but simply coming closer. As the villagers congratulated each other on their powers of observation, several were also excited to note that the shape of the dot was circular.

The dark circle was moving towards the village and it appeared to be followed by two more. The first building these spheres approached was the church, its welcoming lantern shining out in the dark. It was said that each black sphere measured fifteen feet in diameter. They appeared opaque and tangible. But they also seemed able to pass through solid objects; wall, wood, wool and skin.

The first sphere diverted from its straight line as it passed the church and floated towards the lantern. It was this point that the purpose of these spheres was surmised. The dark object flew to the lantern, enveloping it. The light from the lantern faded and disappeared. It didn't sputter or flicker, it just faded away.

The sphere gradually floated around the outside of the church touching every window and as it did so the light from each window turned to grey. The sphere floated back to the street joining its brothers. The villagers noted that it was ever so slightly brighter. It was no longer black, just slightly less black than the other two.

This changed as the spheres progressed through the village; moving through each house, down side streets, and into the square, the lights fading everywhere. As they touched each flame, the spheres slowly brightened. After fifteen minutes the village was in darkness, save for the glow of the three spheres that now appeared to be drawn towards Fylingdales Hall.

The Squire had seen, with members of his horrified household, the progression of the spheres and the trail of darkness that they left in their wake. He ordered more candles to be taken from the storeroom in readiness.

Every fireplace in every room was ignited and at least three candles were placed on every window sill. If Matthew Wilkes had any foresight he would have extinguished all of the lights and let the spheres float on their way, but the squire could not bear the dark. The only way to battle this event was to fight back with light; sweet, safe light.

The braziers that lit the way up to the house were the first to go. One by one the spheres took each light from each flame. They moved closer, encircling the house gradually. With every light swallowed they grew brighter and brighter.

One of the household was standing at the window when the curved edge of a sphere passed through the glass. She saw the light of the flame vanish. When she brought her hand up to touch the wick she found her finger burnt and, on later inspection, black with soot. The flames were still present; it was just the light that had been taken. This was reported from the village too. The villagers had to blow out the blackened flames in case they forgot they were there.

This information never reached the squire. In fact, even if it had, it would have made little difference, obsessed as he was with protecting his family against the dark.

The spheres by now had swallowed all of the light from the windows and outer rooms. Gorged and bursting with light, they made their way into inner chambers and cellars where they took the light from the fires and lanterns within. The squire screamed at his staff to light more fires, but the spheres came for every single one. The spheres were now so bright that, if they had hung two hundred feet above the village, a grandmother with failing eyesight could have read by their light.

As the servants fled into the night, Matthew Wilkes and his family ran to the top floor, huddling together in Jeremiah's bedroom by the final fire. In a panic the squire began to frantically break up chairs. He pulled his sons horsehair mattress to the flames, where, unsurprisingly, a great conflagration began. Strangely the spheres backed away, retreating to the outside of the house where they hung bright and still and shining into the dark. The fire burnt out of control taking the lives of the squire and his family.

The house lit up like a beacon in the night, outshining even the spheres which, when the fire was finally at its brightest, slowly swept in, swallowed the light and let the now black flames consume the house to nothingness.

The three spheres shining brighter than stars floated along the land. They flew back down the street, into the mist, where they dipped behind a hill and set like three little suns.

(NB. In times of mist, villages from all around the Black Meadow light enormous and bright bonfires on the outskirts of their land.

They turn out all the lights in every house and wait for the spheres to come.

These events are called Black Nights.)

And the gentleman his eyes they flashed
As he spied her from his hide ...

Beyond the Moor

A maiden fair who wore all black
A gentleman did chance to meet.
She had a golden pendant there
Plac'd around her neck so sweet.

And the gentleman his eyes they flashed
As he spied her from his hide
And he jump'd upon the lonely girl
And pull'd her to his side.

He said, "Give me that fair pendant girl
Give it now or I shall take
From you that precious treasure
That with a husband you should make."

But the maiden fair she was not scar'd
She did not scream or wail,
She did not bite or kick or punch
Or writhe or twitch or flail.

"Take my pendant if you dare
And take my treasure for
I have no fear of you good sir
As I've been *Beyond the Moor*."

The rogue it seem'd was ta'en aback
As maidens always scream'd,
And for a maid to simply shrug
Was more than he had dream'd

"I shall take your pendant then
And then I shall take more!"
"Take it then," she said and grinn'd
"For I've been *Beyond the Moor.*"

Now this gentleman relaxed his grip
And stood aback and thought;
Why was this maiden not afear'd?
Had she not been taught
That men like him were vile and rough
And would kill you once they'd won
Their prize from you upon the road
And left you all undone?

He told her this but she smil'd again
And he cuff'd her on the jaw.
She laugh'd and said, "Oh cuff away!
For I've been *Beyond the Moor.*"

"You've been *Beyond the Moor*," he said
"And what is in this place
That you don't fear what my sharp blade
Will do to your sweet face?"

But the girl she laugh'd again and said,
"Cut away dear friend
Flay my skin and sear my flesh
It will not be my end.

You cannot harm what is not here
And was not here before,
You cannot harm me little man
For I've been Beyond the Moor."

"Enough of this!" the villain scream'd
"Your wits are gone is all,
The truth that you don't fear your end
Don't mean your end don't call.

So you shall feel this blade's sharp edge
And you shall feel it yet
And I will take your treasure dear
Afore the moon is set."

So he thrust his blade into her chest
And he thrust and twist and tore
But she smil'd and whisper'd once again
"I've been *Beyond the Moor.*"

And he screamed at her and cut again
And thrust his hand in more
And as his hand sank further still
He heard "*Beyond the Moor.*"

He went to pull the blade right out
To make another start
But found his hand and blade stuck fast
Inside her beating heart.

And as it beat, with every pulse
His arm drew further in
To his elbow, shoulder too
Then finally his chin.

He strain'd his neck and look'd at her
And she smil'd again once more
"And when your journey all is done
We'll go *Beyond the Moor*."

And with that, his head was pull'd
Into the gaping scar,
Then his torso, kicking legs
Were dragg'd in deep and far.

And when at last the feet were gone
She look'd down at her chest
And where the cut had just now been
A tear was in her dress.

She brush'd her clothes and smil'd again
A sweet smile, soft and pure.
She tuck'd her pendant safe away
And walk'd *Beyond the Moor*.

A Phenomenal Occurrence

Was it when the air turned white and you couldn't
see your own feet tramping on the ground?
Was it when the sky changed shape and the moon
went from full to half in an eye's blink?
Was it when the seventh child who walked alone
never returned?
Was it the cry of the Rag and Bone Man that
turned my spine to ice?
Was it the taste of the golden apples from the tree
that wasn't there yesterday?
Was it the dance of the Horsemen on the third
night of a warm October?
Was it when the lights grew and I forgot my place
and time?
Was it when she came from the fog house and her
eyes darkened?
Was it the standing stone that stood still, almost
toppled and then took a step?
Or was it when you noticed me?
Was it when you turned your bonny head?
Was it when you flashed your smile and held my
hand?

(Recorded by R. Mullins – Notes VII)

The house was white and seemed, at first glance, to be an image of a house formed from smoke or mist …

The Fog House

On the road through Black Meadow there was a patch of land from which nothing would grow. No farmer could till it, labourers broke their tills upon it and not even moss or lichen could find purchase. Travellers would pass this dry patch of wasteland everyday with nary a sideways glance, but in the village it was known to be much more than dead soil.

When the scream of the Rag and Bone man arose and the fog spread over the meadow, the peculiar was always said to be hot on its heels. One villager spoke of a Fog House that appeared at the side of the road on the patch of barren land. He was walking back towards the village when the mist arose. He knew that he should seek cover swiftly, but the mist came down so fast that he quickly became disorientated. He made sure that he could feel the gravel of the road underneath his feet and moved forward, safe in the knowledge that he remained on the path to the village. He had slowed his pace somewhat, wondering when he would see the lights of the tavern ahead of him, when he noticed a large house looming over him on his right. The house was white. It seemed at first glance, to be an image of a house formed from smoke or mist. But, as the man reached for the fog door handle and he felt the cold metal against his skin, he knew that this was something far more tangible. He thought that his eyes were playing tricks, for although he could feel the hard metal of the handle and the rough wood of the door; to his eyes it still retained the essence of fog or smoke.

Curiosity got the better of him. He entered the Fog House. He found himself in a fog hallway. Looking about he saw that the mist walls were adorned with wispy frames in which the white smoke portraits of lords and ladies hung. He saw that there were fog stairs leading up into the darkness and a passage led down from the front door with several misty rooms branching off it.

If he squinted he could still make out the road through the fog walls, but, when he touched the wall could feel painted plaster under his fingers.
He walked into the first room on the right, marvelling at the fog fire crackling away in the fog fireplace and at the comfortable armchair with its back to him, from which puffs of tobacco smoke plumed up to the fog candelabra with its misty candles and smoke flames.

The man cleared his throat. A figure rose from the armchair. An imposing fog man, with a powdered periwig, fat belly and pipe clamped between his teeth. The figure frowned at the stranger; the wisps of fog that were his eyebrows dancing as his expression altered. When he spoke, his voice was clear, in the same way, the villager was sure, that he would be solid to the touch.

"What is your business in my house, stranger?"

The villager was taken aback but when he regained his composure managed the reply.

"Apologies, sir, I was seeking shelter from the ..."

He tried to search for a word other than "fog", not wishing to draw attention to the fact that he might have found the strange house and its occupant in some way disagreeable or out of the ordinary, so he settled on "weather."

The fog man walked over to the fog window, pulling the fog curtains apart. He looked out into the impenetrable cloud.

"The weather looks fine."

"I thought there was a storm brewing," the man stammered.

"Are you certain?" The fog man looked concerned. "Then of course you must stay."

He clapped his fog hands together. Through the door entered a rotund lady, smiling and jolly. With her was a young maid; beautiful, all smiles and, of course, like her mother and father, composed entirely of fog.

"The gentleman says there is a storm coming," the fog father said to his family. "So naturally I said that he must stay here with us."

The two women smiled but the villager could not take his eyes off their daughter. Despite being made of sweet white mist, she was a truly magnificent sight.

"Father, will the gentleman be joining us for dinner?"

"Of course, my child."

The villager said that he didn't want to be putting this fine family to any trouble. The fog mother tut-tutted saying that she always made too much, pointing at the fat fog belly of her husband to help illustrate the point further.

While the fog mother and daughter prepared the evening meal, the fog father asked the villager about his occupation and background. He told the villager the history of the house, that it was over two hundred years old and that his family had lived there for many generations. All the time the villager battled against the desire to ask whether this family were ghosts or spirits and was just about to do so when the vision that was the fog daughter called them in to dinner.

They sat at the smoke table. The villager gave his chair and the table a wary knock and was satisfied as to their robust quality. The fog mother and daughter brought out fog knives and fog forks and laid fog dishes upon the fog table. Piping hot fog pork chops and fog potatoes with fog gravy were placed upon his plate. The villager prodded the food with his finger, breathing in the oven fresh aromas.

"It must be my eyes," he thought. "I have been out in the fog for so very long that here in this lovely house all I see is fog."

So he tucked into his fog supper, finding it most delicious and filling. The fog man insisted that the villager stay the night and so, after supper was completed, he was shown to his room by the fog daughter. She led the way up the fog stairs holding a fog lantern to light the way. The villager was disconcerted to see the ground so far below his feet as though he were walking across a thin vale of cloud. He could see the fog father sitting once again in his fog armchair, whilst the mother washed the fog dishes in another room.

The fog daughter opened the door to the guest room, smiling shyly as she let the man inside. He looked at the fog bed and nodded appreciatively, commenting on how comfortable it looked. The fog daughter asked whether the villager had a wife. The villager, who did indeed have a wife and three charming children, was struck by a sudden and uncontrollable urge to lie. Pleased that he was unmarried, the maid asked him if he had ever lain with a woman, and he again, so consumed with lust for this fog creature, told her that he was unshamed. The more he stared at the fog daughter, the more he craved her. As she turned to leave she whispered to him to leave his door unlocked and, as her fog lips brushed against his ear, the villager thought that he could dance for joy.

That night when the fog house was dark, the fog daughter came to him. They shared a sweet love sullied only by the lie that had allowed it.

In the morning the man awoke on the cold hard ground of the barren patch of land. There was no sign of the fog daughter who had left his room with a smile, no fat fog father, no jolly fog mother and no fog house. The mist that had led him here had completely disappeared. He could now see the spire of the village church in the distance. He marvelled at the vividness of what he assumed must have been a dream and walked joyfully back home.

He never told his family of his adventure on the way home, why would they need to know about what was probably just a silly dream? However, he did tell his friends in the tavern of his exploits. They all thought the tale worthy of a drink or two. It was a tale worth repeating. The man found that the story kept him in free ale from friends and strangers for many months to come.

But gentlemen gossip just like old wives. The villager's wife soon heard the tale. Though it hurt her deeply she knew it was just a silly dream. It was a hurtful tale of course, but a tale nonetheless. The villager knew nothing of her hurt and continued to tell his story. And still people brought him ale and still he laughed about his silly but vivid dream.

Several months later something occurred that would cause the villager to never tell his tale again. He woke late one morning and looked out of the window to see his wife driving his cart away from the house. Sitting with his wife were his three children sobbing, wailing and looking back at the house with despairing eyes. He flew down the stairs in a panic. Flinging open the door to pursue them, he noticed, there on the doorstep, a little fog basket inside of which, wrapped in mist blankets, was a fog infant mewling and crying for its father.

When the mist spreads
Like an unspooling ball of wool
Threading over the land

When the mist spreads

When the mist spreads
Like an unspooling ball of wool
Threading over the land
Can you see the smoke from the chimneys?
Can you see the roofs above the cloud?
And if the mist rises
If the mist rises
The village will come
The village has come

When the mist has risen
And the clouds fade
The children smile and play their games
But if you ask to join them
If you ask to skip, or hop the scotch
They shake their heads in dismay
"Don't come here
Listen for the cry of the Rag and Bone man"
If you want to sup their ale
Or kiss the pretty maid under the yellow apple tree
They shake their heads in dismay
"Don't come here
Listen for the cry of the Rag and Bone man"

(Recorded by R. Mullins – Notes IX)

And it was this gentleman that the Devil decided to meet one Saturday evening.

The Devil and the Yoked Man

Many of the tales of the Black Meadow try to explain how the world disappears from its borders, how, when the mist comes, the world fades from around the village. Of course, to the world it is the village that vanishes but this is of course a simple matter of perspective.

There was a labourer who enjoyed working the fields. Where others toiled for hours and moaned, he did so with nary a complaint. Where others could not wait to run from the field to the tavern at the end of a long day, he had to be pulled from the field, so determined he was to finish the job for the good of the village. The village was his passion; he loved every corner, every flower pot, and every person. Though others thought his behaviour peculiar, they did not shun him, knowing that his passion was for them and their well-being.

And it was this gentleman that the Devil decided to meet one Saturday evening. All the others had left the field, but the man was still tilling the soil alone having attached the yoke to his shoulders as his ponies had long since retired and gone in to their stables to rest.

"You are working hard," said the Devil who was dressed in a long scarlet robe with a golden clasp. It is said that his face was the most handsome you would ever see, with a smooth shaved chin and tidy locks framing his beautiful visage. But for all his beauty his eyes were hard, cold, black and dead.

The yoked man smiled, grunting in reply, but did not stop. The Devil walked alongside while the yoked man toiled and tried to engage him further in conversation but with no success.

"You work here while others rest and drink in the tavern?"

The Devil searched the yoked man's face but got no response, just that continuing smile.

"Even the horses rest and you are expected to pull the tiller yourself."

Again there was no response, just the smile.

"Surely you want some respite from this ceaseless toil?"

But the yoked man just grinned and pulled harder. The Devil followed, puzzled by the man's keenness for servitude.

"Good sir, will you stop and speak with me a while?"

The yoked man continued to pull, ignoring the devil whose tone was slowly becoming more impatient.

"Good sir, I beg your indulgence for a while, if you will but stop I can give you your heart's desire."

But the yoked man continued to pull. Finally the Devil commanded in a voice that echoed like thunder across the meadow:
"I command you to stop. You will stop and you will listen."

The yoked man tried to pull at the tiller. He attempted to move his feet but found that he could not; he sighed and looked hard at the Devil.

"I want nothing from you," he said. "I need nothing, for honest work is its own reward."

"You are a fool," said the Devil. "You are blind to the delights of the world. I can show you such things that you will scream for joy and beg me to give them to you."

So the Devil brought him a chest larger than a fat giant's coffin. He opened it, revealing jewels and gold beyond the nation's wealth.

"I shall give you this," he smiled.

The yoked man shook his head saying,
"Go away and let me pull."

The Devil frowned and waved his hand. A maid appeared, clad in flowing white, more beautiful than the morning and sweeter than fresh honey

dripping from its comb. The yoked man shook his head, saying for the second time,
"Go away and let me pull."

The lady walked towards the yoked man. A golden palace materialised with one hundred servants all bowing and singing the yoked man's name in glorious harmony. The yoked man spat on the floor, squinted at the Devil and shook his head. The Devil fumed. He clicked his fingers in delight at his new realisation,
"Ah! Do you fear for your soul? Maybe you have heard that Satan gives treasures only in return for this most precious of things? Well that is true, but in this case I shall make an exception. You can have all of these things if you will but stop. I vow to you on Hell and all its dominions. I vow to you on my own demonic blood, on my Unholy Mother and my Holy Father. I vow on The Fall and on the Invert Cross. I vow that I shall not take your beloved soul."

But the yoked man shook his head, saying for the third time,
"Go away and let me pull. What I do, I do for the good of others, for the village, not for myself."

The Devil found a rage growing within him, a rage akin to that he had harboured against his Heavenly Father before The Fall. His dark blood boiled, his eyes blazed fire and his voice shook.
"You will take nothing from me? I who own the night and dance the terrible dance? I who ride the

thunder and eat the misty air? I who cover the sun and howl at the moon? I who drink fresh blood and feast on souls? You dare turn away a gift, not a bargain but a gift, from me? Something I have never offered another mortal in all of human history?"

The yoked man shrugged and said for the fourth time with his own venom in his voice,
"Go away and let me pull."

The Devil was shocked into silence and walked away from the yoked man. The Devil looked out over the village. After a moment he snapped his fingers and turned to face him.

"You work for the good of the village?"

The yoked man nodded.

The Devil smiled.

"That is an honourable thing. For you will work hard then to keep them prosperous?"

The yoked man nodded.

The Devil continued:
"You will work hard to keep the people fed?"

The yoked man nodded.

The Devil said,

"You will work hard to keep the village safe? To keep it out of Hell?"

And as the yoked man nodded the Devil raised his hand. There was a rumble of grinding and tearing from beneath the earth. Cracks appeared in the ground all the way around the village. Smoke and fog erupted from these tiny fissures and the land glowed an angry red. Slowly the village began to sink into the earth.

The Devil waved his hand and the tiller flew from its chains. The chains stretched and grew, snaking their way from the yoke around the labourer's neck towards the sinking village. As the ends of the chains reached the hole, they flew down, plunging into the earth by the church, deep into the rock underneath the village, deeper and deeper until they were stuck fast.

The yoked man found his feet slipping and sliding under him as the weight of the village pulled him down to Hell with it. But when all seemed lost and he was tottering near the edge of the abyss, one of his feet found purchase. He pulled at the yoke and the village stopped its descent.

The Devil laughed.

"How long can you hold on my friend? You may bring the village back up to the waking world but it will always drag you down again. Sometimes you may hold it for a few weeks or days or for one night, but then it shall be gone again and you with it. Can you do this? Can you do this for all eternity?"

The yoked man looked at the Devil, saying with a smile,
"Go away and let me pull."

And the Devil went away and the yoked man pulled.

He was shocked to see that where the dwellings of workers once stood that young trees burst through the shattered rooftops.

The Long Walk to Scarry Wood

One day, hundreds of years ago, a man had to make a journey from the village of Badger Wood across the meadow to a place known as Scarry Wood. Most people would take the road around the Black Meadow to get there. This was not due to any superstition about the area, but because the path was treacherous; spotted as it was with dips, holes and swamp. The man had been tasked with getting to the Scarry Wood Log Mill within one day to deliver new timber orders for his Squire's outhouses. He was considered the fastest of all the Squire's men, so bid his wife and three children farewell and began the six-mile walk. He would be back by the end of the day. The Squire even gave him a groat so he could eat at the Black Meadow Inn on the way.

It was midway through a bitterly cold March. The flowers were cautiously peeking out of hedgerows and the cracks in the ground, whilst insects were just beginning to hum.

As he approached the edge of the Black Meadow, he happened upon an old gentleman slowly pulling at a rickety wooden cart, loaded with sacks of grain. The old gentleman was clearly struggling, so the traveller asked if he required assistance. The old gentleman was pleased, telling him that he was making for the farm just a furlong down the road.

As they saw the slate roofs of the farm buildings in the near distance, the rain began to come down. The traveller and the old man remarked to each other that they had never seen a downpour like it. Puddles formed swiftly. Little rivers ran down the path towards them, turning the ground beneath their feet to soft, sticky and deep mud. Finding their boots and the wheels of the cart becoming stuck, they fought to pull the cart along, but it was all to no good. The traveller decided to get some help to pull the cart and its heavy sacks of grain from the mud. The old gentleman's feet were stuck fast. The mud was rapidly rising to his knees. The old gentleman waved the traveller away when he offered to pull him out, telling him that his time would be better spent getting help. The traveller squelched his way out of the mire and ran across the field to the farm.

As he crossed the field, the rain suddenly stopped. He found himself running in the blazing and surprisingly warm sunshine. On reaching the farm he was surprised to find it silent. In fact, on reflection, the field he ran through did seem uncared for and overgrown. He wondered whether the old gentleman had made a mistake. He ran from building to building, calling out for help but got no response. He noticed that shutters were broken, doors were hanging off their hinges, and tiles were missing from the roofs. The farm, from its buildings to the surrounding fields, seemed utterly neglected. Had the old gentleman meant to come here? He walked to the main house and opened the front door. Inside it was completely empty. There were no tables or chairs. It was a shell. He ran up the stairs. There were no beds in any of the chambers. Realising he would get no help here, he quickly ran to one of the barns and was pleased to find some rope which he took back to the old gentleman at speed.

He called out to the old gentleman as he approached but got no reply. When he got there he saw that the ground was dry and solid, with no indication that it had rained. There was no sign of the old gentleman or the cart. As he searched about, calling the old gentleman's name, he saw in a ditch, by the side of the road, the remains of an old cart wheel. It was much like the old gentleman's, but this one was rotten, with fungus and moss covering its broken spokes. It could not be the same wheel. After an hour of searching the path, ditch and surrounding trees, the traveller decided to continue his journey to Scarry Wood.

He had lost a lot of time helping the old gentleman, so he ran along the path. After a short while he reached the village in the centre of the Black Meadow. He had visited this village once before on another errand for his Squire, many years previously and had considered it just like any other, but today the people seemed strange. They wore clothes of a different style to his, where he wore a leather jerkin, breeches and a rough woollen shirt; the men were clad in white shirts and black coats. Their clothes seemed smart, rich and light. The ladies, in their long black skirts, wore white caps upon their heads, fixed by a tie under their chins. The traveller wondered whether they were having some sort of celebration or carnival which would cause them to wear such strange clothes, but it was clear that these people were going about their daily business as though nothing was out of the ordinary.

The carts in the village were of a much better design than those of Badger Wood. Feeling hungry and realising it must be long past noon, he walked to the building that he knew to be the tavern, but found it locked. Its unfamiliar neat glass windows with crisscross black lead piping, had boards nailed across them. He turned from the door and saw a few people looking at him and tut-tutting.

Seeing that he would find no succour there, the traveller continued on his way. It was early evening by the time he reached the Scarry Wood Log Mill. The path was overgrown and the Log Mill little more than a ruin. He had been there the previous year. It had been a thriving business, providing timber for houses and farms for miles around. The place was in utter disrepair. There were no frames in the windows, let alone glass. The mortar was crumbling, parts of some of the buildings had fallen down and the roof had collapsed in the main building. As he entered the shell, a deer cantered past him before jumping through the remains of a window in the ruins of what was once a busy and prosperous mill.

The traveller tried to fathom what had happened and what he should do about it. Who was he to give the contracts to? He wandered around the perimeter of Scarry Wood to make sure that he had come to the right place. He was shocked to see that where the dwellings of workers once stood, young trees now burst through the shattered rooftops. The houses stood in disrepair, roofs mossy and windows gone. He listened. There was no sound of any human activity at all, only birdsong. He wondered what his master would make of the situation. He had expected to stay the night in the workers' quarters at Scarry Wood Log Mill, but, as that now stood in ruins, even the floors having long since rotted away and disappeared, he knew that he would have to find shelter elsewhere. So he made up his mind to throw himself at the mercy of the people of the village in the centre of the Black Meadow. Even if they didn't have a tavern, surely someone would take pity on a footsore and weary traveller.

It was already dark by the time he got there but the village was alive with sound and music. As he walked through the village he noted that there seemed to be more houses than there were earlier that day. Not only that, but these houses were of a strange and distinct style. They were tall and joined together with no thatch upon the roof. To add to his confusion he heard the sound of laughter and music coming from the abandoned tavern. The place seemed to be the centre of the village. A roar of laughter echoed out as the door slammed open. A gentleman in a rich purple coat with a short white wig atop his head, staggered out with a powdered woman on his arm. The traveller gasped at the change, staring wide-eyed at the buildings, the clothes and the people. As he gaped at all the changes, a cold chill clutched at his heart. He felt an urge to get home as swiftly as he could. On his exit from the village, he glanced up at the brazier that marked the boundary, but it had been replaced by a smart metal pole, on top of which a glass case held a bright burning flame that seemed to have no wick or candle base.

He ran as fast as his legs would allow, passing the farm, which from the road he could hear the sounds of livestock and see lights in the windows. It was not the abandoned ruin he had seen in the morning.

What would have happened to his home?

He paused after passing the ditch where he had seen the Old Gentleman's cartwheel. He noticed that the road was no longer a dirt track. Instead it had a smooth surface. As he bent down to examine it by the light of the rising sun, he heard a high-pitched scream coming out of the darkness. It seemed to be coming from the east. As he looked out, he saw a plume of smoke in the middle distance running along the ground at great speed. Following it were tiny squares of light, grouped together in rectangular box shapes. The traveller moaned, turning on his heel from the monster, and ran home.

He reached the entrance to his village and sprinted to his house, but could not find it, the streets had changed shape ... The church hall had been replaced by a brick barn. Where his own home had been, was now a row of small red-brick cottages, all joined together, sporting large windows and doors of different colours. He heard a strange buzzing noise above his head. Looking up he saw an enormous bird with four wings, two on either side of its massive body. The wings were stiff and did not flap. He watched open mouthed as it flew out of sight.

It was at that point that a villager came out of one of the red-brick houses. He asked, in a strange and almost incomprehensible dialect, if the traveller needed help. The traveller, weeping, was acutely aware that this stranger was looking at his clothes in curiosity. He told the man that he was lost and wanted to go home although he could not find it. He described his house through his rising sobs but the stranger from the red-brick house looked at him blankly.

On seeing how distraught the traveller was, the stranger from the red-brick house asked his name and on learning that it was "Kirby" suddenly laughed. The traveller was puzzled by this response to the mention of his name and demanded an explanation. The villager begged apology for any offence, pointing at the sign at the start of the street which read "Kirby Lane". The villager explained that it was named after a traveller who went missing 400 years previously, leaving his wife and family to ponder his fate.

The traveller put a hand to his mouth and, stifling a sob, ran from the village back into the arms of the Black Meadow. He was never seen again.

Though, if you wait long enough, maybe *you* will see him.

The Scarry Wood Lament

So long
I have walked so long
It seems like an hour
But it could be a day

All my life I've been waiting
To take a step upon the road
Walk away from the home that I love
And see the sun shining in a sky so far away

So long
I have walked so long
It seems like an hour
But it could be a year

All the faces along the path
Are changing as I pass
The children now are old and dear
And now my home is far from my grasp

So long
I have walked so long
It seems like an hour
But it could be forever

(Traditional)

His choice of subject remained the same: the standing stone in the centre of the meadow.

The Stone Steps

An artist came to Black Meadow in the spring and autumn of every year. Those who asked what brought him back were told that it was "the light, my dears, the light."

He worked primarily in oils and, after a breakfast at the local tavern, would stick two blank canvases under his arm and venture out into the meadow.

He hailed from the south and was, on his first visit, unused to the changeable weather, but on his succeeding journeys he wore a thick coat and fine tough leather boots that kept out the wet. He was a man of considerable private means who held himself well and was assumed to be a proper London gentleman. His choice of subject remained the same: the standing stone in the centre of the meadow. A stark grey monolith peppered with ancient-looking spirals carved into its granite hide. Most houses in the village had one of his paintings adorning a wall, the tavern boasted several.

This peculiar tale begins when the gentleman made his tenth visit to the village. It was autumn and he came to the tavern eager to capture an image of the Standing Stone caught in the blaze of vernal sunrise. On his first morning - after he had eaten heartily - he packed up his easel, two canvases, and his box of paints. He gratefully took the cold lunch prepared by his landlady and walked into the twilight before the dawn.

On his return he seemed quiet and thoughtful, not upset, but preoccupied by a sudden thought. Something of magnitude was weighing upon his brow, but he would not share it with any of the villagers, with whom he was often most open and gregarious.

At the end of the second day his funk seemed more pronounced. He escaped to his room without any supper, muttering about his sketches. When the landlady visited his room to offer him a hot drink, she found the room covered in scattered pictures and the artist poring over old drawings in a sketch pad.

On the third day he ran out without a breakfast morsel passing his lips. So eager was he that the landlady was still in her nightdress and was only just starting her own morning ablutions. It was on his return that his behaviour became more erratic. He slammed the tavern door wide open, walking straight over to the four paintings of the Standing Stone that hung above the bar. He peered at his creations furiously for some minutes. He stood on a bar-stool, took them from the wall and laid them side by side on the table. The artist stared at them for a long while, muttering to himself about dates and measurements. After what seemed an age, he lifted his head and ran from the inn.

His actions were the talk of the village the next day. He had visited every house in the village, hammered upon every door, barged in, pulled his paintings from their walls and left without a thank you. He brought over twenty-five paintings back to the tavern and began to lay them upon the largest table there. When it was clear that they did not fit, he pushed the table to the side, cleared stools and chairs, asking anybody drinking to move from his way. He laid the pictures side by side on the floor. He muttered and cursed as the landlady and her customers looked on in bemusement. He moved the pictures around, shaking his head. He adjusted the positions of each painting, until, after half an hour of shifting one to the left and three to the right, two here and four there; rotating, lifting, swapping and changing, he finally stopped and stood back, seemingly satisfied.

"Look!" he shouted. "Look! Can't you see? The stone steps!"

The villagers crowded around, peering with great interest at his paintings. Each picture showed the Standing Stone at different times of day, in different seasons. They commented on his excellent use of colour, on his shading, his masterful stroke and the realism of his pictures, but none of them understood his meaning.

"The stone steps!" he said again. "The stone steps!"

Early the next morning the gentleman went from door to door and returned the pictures to their owners with heartfelt apologies for his intrusions and rudeness. Nobody seemed to mind, putting the whole strange incident down to the eccentricities of an artist.

He was back to himself the following day; smiling, happy and ebullient. He did not visit the stone, but instead spent the morning tidying away the papers that he had scattered and the afternoon eating and drinking with the villagers. The next day he left for London with a promise that he would return soon.

The Artist's visits increased over the next five years, arriving now at the change of *every* season. Every day he would go and paint, but, to the disappointment of the villagers, he kept all the works to himself. In the spring of the eleventh year since he first arrived at the public house, the Artist announced that he would be displaying his works in the village hall. There was a great clamour and excitement from the villagers, which doubled on the announcement that visitors from the capital would also be coming to see.

The visitors were an eclectic troupe. There were a few artists, an art critic, some scholarly-looking gentlemen and a journalist or two. On the night of the exhibition the villagers chatted and laughed with excitement about their eccentric artist, wondering at what would be revealed.

The first reaction to the exhibition was one of bewilderment. The villagers gawked at the pictures in disbelief. There were over two hundred paintings, in the same style, from the same perspective, all of the standing stone. Some laughed, some whispered, but many were silent; sad at the Artist's folly. He was a popular man and they did not want to see him ridiculed.

The visitors at first also seemed overwhelmed by the repetitive nature of the exhibition, but gradually, as they examined the pictures, the mood in the Village Hall changed. The villagers felt it too. They found themselves scrutinising the paintings more closely than before. They walked, peered at every detail and compared notes on what they had discovered. They ran, moving from picture to picture, to check, to make sure that, "No, it couldn't be ..." and "Surely not ..." But yes, little by little, painting by painting there it was; the stone moving slowly across the landscape.

"Impossible!" they cried. "A trick!"

But they knew the artist was no liar. They remembered that night when he had seen the phenomenon himself for the first time. They remembered his realisation: "The Stone steps," he had said. And now with so much effort, with so much patience, he had proved it to be true and at last they understood what he had meant.

The Seventh Child

Your first is a china cup and you do everything the elders tell you. Not too much, not too little, not too hot, not too cold, not too tight, not too soft. You remember every smile, every word, every step.

Your second is perfect, for you have learnt from your errors. You know how much, how little, how hot, how cold, how tight, how soft. You remember nearly everything.

The third is ignored. You do not mean to, but you know all now and so should the third.

The fourth is brought up by the first and the second.

The fifth is a surprise and you start to treat them as the first, swearing that you will do better this time. But then you grow weary and treat them as the third.

The sixth is not like the others. The sixth makes trouble but the sixth is your favourite. The sixth needs nothing. The sixth takes everything.

And the seventh?
The seventh child?
The seventh child wanders.
The seventh child drifts.
The seventh child shall break your heart.

The old woman stood outside, behind the gate, looking at the house.

The Meadow Hag

The farmer had been meaning to repair the wall around the well for months. The hole sat in the centre of an overgrown field just outside the village. He had finished rounding up his sheep and was walking back to the lights of the farmhouse, in the deepening dusk, when he heard the cry.

It made him stop. The cry was low and almost indistinct. He stood still, tilted his head and listened. The sheep were shuffling and bleating lightly as they settled for the night. A soft wind tickled the browning leaves into a series of whispering rustles. Under that sound, in the distance was the cry. The farmer did not hesitate; it was clearly coming from the well. He ran to its edge and peered down into the darkness.

"Hello?" he called "Are you hurt?"

A groan was the only reply.

The farmer acted swiftly. He secured the well rope and removed the bucket before lowering himself down into the darkness. The twilight of the evening gave little detail inside the well, but he could just make out what looked like a large bundle of rags next to his feet as he reached the bottom. The farmer squatted down and patted the bundle which shifted under his hand and gave a little cough.

He lifted the bundle to his shoulder and was surprised at its weight. It felt as though he was carrying a pair of downy pillows, albeit ones with sharp corners and bone-like protrusions. He made sure that his cargo would not fall and climbed back up without difficulty.

Once in the open he lowered the body onto the grass and rolled it over. He was taken aback by the appearance of this old woman. She was clothed in what looked like old hessian sacks. Her hands were so long and the skin so tight on each crooked digit that they resembled the desiccated claws of a dead cockerel. But it was her face that provoked the most visceral reaction. He stared at her visage and could not control his shivering. Her face was so wrinkled and so full of lines that it looked as though it had been scribbled upon by an angry child.

The old woman's eyes flickered open. She smiled; her wrinkles cracking and shifting to meet the demands of the muscles in her face. The farmer helped her to her feet.

"How does it fare with you, lady?"

The old woman checked herself over.

"I took a mighty tumble, dear sir, and I feared all was lost."

The farmer told her to walk carefully from now on and she assured him that she would. The farmer smiled and turned to go but the old woman put a hand on his arm. He stopped and she spoke.

"I want to show my thanks."

The farmer could see that this was a woman of little means.

He said, "You be sure to tread carefully so I don't have to fish you out of any more holes. That will be thanks enough."

The old lady shook her head.

"I give you my protection. As you saved me from harm so I save you."

"That is very kind," smiled the farmer, laughing inwardly at the thought that this frail old creature could protect him from anything at all.

He doffed his cap and gave a small bow. After the lady returned the gesture he walked back home.

It was as he turned the corner to walk the final track to his house that he glanced behind him and saw, in the distance, the old woman standing and watching. He waved at her and continued on.

As the farmer opened the gate into the yard he saw the old woman again, standing, watching him. He waved again, walked across the yard and stepped into his house.

The farmer's wife kissed him in welcome as he crossed the kitchen floor to embrace her. She asked him of his day, of his travails and whether he had eaten the bread and cheese that she had secreted inside his pouch. He smiled and stroked her head, thanking his wife for the small ale that she placed there that had warmed him when he had taken of his noon victuals.

His wife was his light, his whole life. He gazed upon her as she placed a bowl of delicious lamb stew in front of him. They ate silently together; he enjoying the sight of her, whilst she revelled in the sounds of his contentment as he wolfed down the stew.

When he pushed his bowl away he told her of his adventure. She listened rapt and proud as he recounted how he had rescued the old lady.

"Was she well?" his wife asked.

"I left her standing and with no bone broken."

"She was lucky that you were passing."

"She was grateful," smiled the farmer in recollection.

"She offered me her protection to repay my kindness!"

His wife laughed heartily at this. Her husband was so strong, so lithe, so full of health, so fast and so brave; he was not a man who needed help or any sort of protection at all. The husband stopped her laughing as she saw a grave look darken his face.

"I would swear that she was following me home. She was a long way behind, but when I turned I could see her."

The wife laughed again, took up the dishes and walked to the sink. She looked out of the window and stopped. She gave a little gasp, waving her husband to her side.

The old woman stood outside, behind the gate, looking at the house.

"She followed me!" marvelled the farmer.

"She will catch a chill, husband."

The farmer was a good man. He looked at his wife and nodded. Once outside he saw that the woman was still by the gate staring at him. She did not budge as he approached.

"Will you come inside?"

She shook her head.

"My wife has made a stew."

She shook her head again, whispering, "I give you my protection."

"I insist, please come inside."

The old lady relented and followed the farmer into his house. The farmer's wife poured out a generous portion of lamb stew from the pot into a bowl and put it on the table. The old woman who was still standing at the door looked at the stew.

"Please eat," said the farmer's wife.

The old lady looked at her.

"Please sit down and eat," the farmer said.

The old woman sat down and brought the bowl to her lips. She opened her mouth, poured the stew inside and seemed to swallow it down in a single gulp. She stood and made to leave. The wife - astonished by the old woman's appetite - was silent, but the farmer, having seen more than his fair share of strange sights, was still hospitable.

"Do you have a place to stay?"

The old woman nodded.

"I do sir, but you are under my protection."

"I assure you good lady that I do not need it."

"And yet you have it. It is not a gift, sir. It is not given freely, you have earned my protection by your works and my protection you have."

The farmer smiled at her determination.

"Will you not relent? I assure you I need no protection."

"Bless you, sir," said the old woman. "You rescued me from darkness and peril. You plucked me from the jaws of death. You see before you an old woman, wrinkled and ancient, a hag who surely has nothing to give you. But I give you my protection. You have it."

The farmer's wife was starting to feel discomfited by this old crone's passion and whispered,
"The hour is late, Husband, and the animals will need their feed early in the morning. We must abed."

The farmer, who knew his wife well, understood her meaning, "Indeed my wife speaks wisely. Will you need accompanying home?"

The old lady shook her head and walked to the door. She turned, looking the farmer in the eye.

"Remember, I bless you, good sir. You are defended."

"Thank you, good lady. Get home safely."

They watched as she walked to the gate. They waved as she undid the latch and stepped from the yard into the darkness. Once the door was closed and they were sure that she was out of earshot, they both laughed long and hard, gripping their sides, holding each other, talking of the woman's strange ways and her powers of protection. Tears streaming and gasping for breath they scrambled upstairs to bed.

The farmer awoke in the night to make his toilet and glanced out of the window on the landing. He shrunk back: there was the woman looking up at him intently, her dull eyes blazing black from beneath her wrinkled brows.

The famer did not sleep and rolled out of bed before the crow of the cock. He went to give the animals their feed half an hour earlier than usual.

And there, standing at the gate, was the old woman. She watched him steadily as he went about his business. He did not know how to react to her. He did not approach or smile or look directly at her. This was too strange to be acknowledged. He could sense her at all times. When he went into the cowshed to begin milking, he hoped that, on his exit, she would be gone. As he came out of the barn he breathed a sigh of relief as he could no longer see her at the gate.

He felt a breath at his shoulder and turning, his heart stopped momentarily, as the old lady was now standing at the door.

"What do you want, madam?"

"To protect you," she replied.

"I need no protection."

"Nonetheless, you are protected."

The farmer turned from the old woman and walked to the farmhouse. In the kitchen his wife was preparing the breakfast. When her husband entered she was startled to see his troubled look.

"The lady is still in the yard."

The farmer's wife rushed to the window and peeked out. Sure enough, there she was, the old woman, behind the gate, staring at the house.

"Why has she not left?"

"I think she has been there all night."

The farmer shook his head.

"I am beginning to wish that I hadn't pulled her from the well."

"She is just a harmless old woman," smiled the farmer's wife. "What can she do?"

The farmer went about his daily chores. He walked his sheep to new pastures and all the time the old woman watched, ready. He fed his chickens and picked one for slaughter. All the while the old woman watched. He went to speak to his labourers who were ploughing the cornfield and was embarrassed that all the way through their conversation the old woman watched. As he walked home she followed and watched. As he sat at his table eating his wife's beautiful stew, with little appetite, he knew that she was outside, watching.

This became a pattern over the next few weeks. He and his wife grew used to the old woman. She became something of a joke with the labourers; they called her "The Farmer's Mistress" and laughed as she followed the farmer about. But she ignored them, never looked at them, and followed the farmer.

The farmer and his wife found it harder to ignore her when he found himself with a cold in the head that developed into a fever. The farmer's wife would not let him rise and went downstairs to make him a soothing posset. She found the old woman standing at the stove cooking up the same herself. The farmer's wife asked the old woman to leave but got no response. She resolved to get the woman out once she had delivered her own posset to her ailing husband.

The farmer's wife worked swiftly boiling up the posset, but the old woman, who had begun first, was already pouring it from the pan into a bowl. The old woman turned from the stove and began to walk to the stairs. The farmer's wife called for her to stop, but the old woman did not falter, so she ran from the stove and blocked her way.
"Thank you for your concern, good lady, but it is a wife's duty to care for her husband. Let me take that posset to him."

The old woman stopped, squinting at the young wife for a moment. She nodded, handing the bowl to her. The farmer's wife thanked the old woman, who left the kitchen and walked to her usual position beyond the gate. Filled with resolve, the farmer's wife walked to the sink and poured the posset down the drain. She rinsed the bowl and refilled it with her own steaming brew from the pan. She took this upstairs and her husband drank it down weakly, slow sip after slow sip.

But as day passed into night, her husband's fever grew worse and his breathing became laboured, the fluid in his cough having sunk to his lungs. She made more posset and remedy but to no avail.

As night deepened she lay next to her husband holding him close to stop his incessant shivering.

She woke with a start to find the moonlight shining through the break in the curtains and her husband sitting up in bed sipping at a fresh bowl of posset.

There, perched in her favourite rocking chair was the old woman, watching him intently.

"What do you want?"

The old woman turned her head slowly to the wife and said, "To help."

The farmer's wife rose from her bed shaking with rage.

"Be gone from my house hag, be gone and do not return! My husband has me and that is all he needs!"

The old woman smiled and asked the farmer, who was looking at his wife in alarm, how he felt.

"I feel fine. In fact I feel better than I have felt in a long time. Your posset has worked wonders, dear wife."

The wife looked at her husband in surprise. The old woman spoke.

"I have given your husband your posset, ma'am. You were asleep and needed your rest so I brewed a posset much like yours and restored him."

The wife sunk back onto the bed and forced a smile.

"Thank you," she muttered.

"Not at all," said the old woman. "I will let you get your rest."

The old woman stood up and left the room, leaving the chair creaking slowly back and forth in the darkness.

The farmer put his bowl on the bedside table and lay down.

"I'm still cold," he said to his wife. "Please hold me."

But the farmer's wife was still in a rage and her vision ran scarlet before her eyes. She lay down and turned her back on her husband; silent tears welling in her open eyes, forming and flowing onto the pillow.

She lay there for a while, waiting for sleep to come, listening to the chattering teeth of her husband and wondering what she should do about this hag from the meadow. The first thing she reasoned, after a while more, was not to turn her back on her husband. He was not at fault; it was his goodness that had brought them to this pass. So she rolled over and went to put her arms around her husband. As her arms began to reach over his frame, she immediately recoiled. Something large was clamped upon him; she could feel rough cloth beneath her hand and sharp pointed bones.

She jumped from the bed. Her hand flew to her mouth in horror as she surveyed the scene. Her husband lay asleep and peaceful; his shivering ended and his teeth chattered no more. But, atop of his slumbering form, holding him in a tight embrace was the Meadow Hag; her wrinkled face close to his, her arms enveloping him, her legs wrapped around him like a young lover or a hound in the fit of heat. Filled with revulsion and a desperate urge to free her husband from this wrinkled carbuncle, the farmer's wife ran to the bed and tried to pull this wizened attachment from her husband's body. But she would not budge.

"Remove yourself!" she demanded, her eyes blazing in a fury.

The old woman seemed to respond to this by holding on all the tighter. The farmer's wife pulled again at the hag's withered body but she held on even tighter, causing her sleeping husband to emit a comforted moan of warm contentment.

The farmer's wife looked about wildly and saw a broom in the corner. She grabbed it quickly, pushing the end of the handle into the space between the Meadow Hag's wrinkled chest and her own husband. She twisted and turned and pulled and pushed but could not remove the old woman from her husband. In frustration she swiftly extracted the pole, raising it above her head ready to strike. As she brought it down with full force, the Meadow Hag's arm shot up, grabbing the handle in her withered claw.

She raised her wrinkled frame from the farmer, pulling the broom from the wife's hand. Standing upon the bed, she held the broom in both hands and snapped it like a dry old twig.

The farmer slept on.

With shocking suddenness and atrocious ferocity the Meadow Hag rained blow after blow onto the head, neck and shoulders of the farmer's wife with the jagged ends of the broken broomstick. The farmer's wife cried out for help but her husband slept on. The Meadow Hag leapt from the bed. She stood over the shuddering frame of the beaten woman. One half of the broom handle dropped to the floor. With her free hand she reached down, thrust her fingers into the wife's beautiful auburn hair and pulled back her head. Ignoring the pleas and cries of terror she pulled back her arm, thrusting the jagged end of the broomstick into the wife's mouth, causing her to gag and choke and flail. She pushed harder, forcing the shaft up inside the wife's head, so her eyes bulged blood and all thoughts stopped forever. Once the convulsions had ceased and the breathing had stopped the Meadow Hag pulled out the handle with a hideous squelch and the wife dropped to the floor.

By the light of the moon, the Hag began to undress; taking off her hessian shawl, her ragged brown dress, petticoat after petticoat, rolling down coarse woollen stockings, until she stood naked, bent, crooked and dry.

She walked to the farmer's wife and with little effort bent down, picked her up and carried her gently over to the bed. The Meadow Hag kissed her bulging eyes and they sank back and shut. She kissed the bruises and cuts from her brutal attack and they faded and closed. Slowly and carefully she removed the wife's nightdress and stared at the still naked form. The Meadow Hag climbed upon the bed and sat on chest of this beautiful corpse. She leant forward and put her hand in the wife's mouth. The Meadow Hag began to shake.

The farmer slept on.

As she trembled, she thrust her other hand into the corpse's mouth until her bony fingers found the hole that the broom handle had made. The trembling increased. A great noise of bones cracking and joints grinding rent the air. The Meadow Hag screamed in pain as her hand drew deeper inside the wife's head and her form grew smaller and slimmer and slighter and shorter still and drew her deeper into the skull of the peaceful corpse. Minutes passed. The screaming and cracking and grinding reached a cacophonic crescendo before diminishing into silence. A pair of tiny wrinkled feet disappeared between the parted lips of the farmer's wife. Her dead mouth snapped shut. The Meadow Hag could not be seen.

The farmer slept on.

After an hour had passed the farmer's wife rose from the bed and looked down at herself by the light of the moon. She put on her nightdress, lay down and embraced her husband, who gave a comforted moan of warm contentment.

Everyone commented on how well and how rested the farmer looked when he returned to work the next day. As the weeks passed, some did comment that his wife seemed quieter, but the people of the village held them up as a paragon of marriage, for they seemed so content and healthy and in love. They whispered about children and at last in the next summer the wife's belly started to bulge and over the next few years the brood grew to an impressive size. Indeed the farmer and his wife lived a long and happy life. The farmer lived to be ninety-seven, which was unheard of in those days. When his grandson asked him what their secret was, the farmer gave a cheerful reply.
"A loving wife and a warm belly."

Everyone commented on how elegant the farmer's wife looked at her husband's funeral. She stood silent and still, her grandson by her side. Before he could react, she leaped down into the grave and lay down upon the coffin. Her grandson ran forward and begged her to climb out, but instead she stood and coughed once into her hand. She smiled, telling her grandson to hold out his hand, which he dutifully did. She dropped a small red seed into his open palm.

"Take this to the well in the lower field," she said, and lay down upon the coffin.

The grandson ran over to the gravediggers for help, but, as he did so, the pile of earth at the side began to tremble and shake and the earth flew into the open grave covering the farmer's wife swiftly. The gravediggers frantically dug away but found nothing but the coffin. Upon opening it, they found the lifeless forms of the farmer and his wife locked in a tight embrace. A doctor was called, but he just shrugged. The magistrate was summoned, but he just shook his head. So they called for the priest, who prayed as they closed up the grave for good.

The next week the farmer's grandson took the red seed to the well in the field, casting it within, sobbing and shaking his head. He sold the farm several years later to a local man who was keen to take on such a property. The grandson was sick of farming and was happy to leave it behind.

A good few years passed and the new farmer was doing a roaring trade. His cows were the talk of the district and he ran an excellent dairy. His farm was prosperous and safe. He was happy for people to wander across the meadows and had, for that reason, filled in the dangerous old well. In its place he planted a beautiful pear tree that bore the most delicious fruit.

It was in the spring, some twenty years later, that this farmer's son noticed that one of the pears was distinctly large and its skin light brown and rough and coarse to the touch. He called his father over and they peered closely into the branches of the tree.

"It will fall," said the farmer. "It will fall."

The other pears seemed untouched by this blight. They waited for it to fall, surprised by its size and keen to see just how large it would grow. But fall it did not, though grow it did, every day larger and larger, most of it light brown and coarse like hessian but a few parts pink and wrinkled. Work in the dairy and at the market kept them away from the pear tree for several weeks.

The farmer's son, walking his dog through the meadow a month later, heard a faint cry and was astonished to see a wrinkled old lady perched on a branch.

"How did you get up there?" he cried.

"Help an old lady down."

The young man assured her that he would and immediately went to fetch a ladder. On his return he climbed up, took the old woman's hands, threw her over his shoulder and brought her safely to the ground.

She thanked him profusely and told him that in return for his good deed he would have her protection. He smiled, thanked her and walked back to the farm, not noticing that she was following at some distance behind.

If either of them had turned around and looked at the pear tree more closely, they would have seen three more large hessian pears on the branches; rough hessian pears with a few parts pink and wrinkled.

The Cry of the Coalman

The snowflakes are hanging
In the air
Nothing's moving
Nothing there

And I want to
Hold your hand
Make you see me
Not just see
Not just see through me

But you're still
And you're so cold
And nothing moves
Not at all

I can't hold you
Touch you
Know you'll see me
Know you'll see me

(Recorded by Roger Mullins at The Old Plough in 1963)

*... in the distance, by the well, he saw a figure with skin
dripping black oil ...*

The Coalman and the Creature

A kindly coalman visited Black Meadow every month during autumn, winter and spring. An old grey pony pulled his rickety cart. He went from house to house, pouring coal down the hatches at the front of every home. He exchanged pleasantries with the ladies who poked their heads from the doors as he passed. Sometimes he would be given a cup of tea, a dry biscuit or a slice of cold ham that he would drink, munch and chew on the front step of a house whilst watching the children play "Hop the Scotch" or "Chase the Hoop" or "Alley of the Hard Foot". He would laugh as they hopped, smile as they chased and wince as they sustained a painful blow whilst running between the two rows of vicious kicking children.

It was in late February and the children were out playing in the snow. They cast great snowballs and flung them at one another. They pulled each other up and down the street on makeshift sleds made of their mothers' tea trays or pot lids. The coalman nudged his pony along the street, pausing as two children slid in front of him. He carefully walked the cart around an enthusiastically made but poorly constructed snowman. He brushed the snow off a cellar hatch, opened it up and began to shovel coal inside.

It was then that he noticed the silence. It was deep and eerie; there was no sound of wind, not a sound of the children, nothing. He turned from his task and looked down the street. A snowball hung in mid-air just inches from a red-headed girl's button nose. The girl herself was shutting her eyes preparing for the impact. A boy was leaning precariously forward; both feet off the ground, seemingly frozen mid-fall. The coalman's pony was completely still, its normally twitching ears utterly lifeless.

The coalman stepped into the street and stared around him in silent wonder.

In the distance, by the well he saw a figure with skin dripping black oil, big bright yellow eyes burning, staring at the red-headed girl. The Coalman watched as this creature began to walk through the street. It ignored the falling boy. It ignored the pony and the coalman. Instead it walked straight to the girl about to be hit by the snowball. The Coalman stared, transfixed, as the creature put its hand on the girl's forehead. The girl shuddered, and while her face drained of colour so the creature's hide, dripping black oil, shone even brighter. The creature turned and, as the Coalman watched, it slithered back to the well, throwing itself over the side.

The Coalman ran to the well and looked down. As his eyes searched the darkness of the shaft, the noises of the village street returned. The Coalman instantly whipped around and saw the little girl with red hair on the ground, her face covered in snow.

The villagers wept for a week. The boy who threw the snowball was taken away by the Sheriff and presented before the Squire who, in his wisdom, declared the girl's death to be a tragic accident born out of the high jinks of children in the snow. She had tripped and hit her head on the ground.

The Coalman did not tell of what he saw. He did not think that he would be believed, for he did not believe it himself and he had seen it. He had seen all go still; he had seen the oil-dripping creature touch that girl's head. He had seen it, but he did not believe it.

He was on his rounds the following month and walked with some trepidation into the village. The children were inside the school. He noticed that when they came out to play, they sat quietly at the side of the street; they did not jump up, did not play and did not laugh. The Coalman grabbed his shovel and moved a heavy load into the Tavern Cellar. The school bell rang, abruptly ceasing as the street was plunged into silence. The Coalman looked about him. He saw the Priest coming out of the church frozen in a gesture of greeting to the Milkmaid across the way, and as he peered closer he could see that the Milkmaid's face was stuck in a coy smile. He saw the children frozen in their sad exodus from the street into their classroom. He saw the creature again, standing by the well, black oil dripping from its bloated frame.

The kindly Coalman gripped the handle of his shovel tightly and ran towards the creature, his voice raised in a battle cry. He brought his shovel down upon the head and shoulders of the creature; it gave a soft cry, an almost human cry of pain. He hit it again and again and again yelling in fury and disgust, ignoring the black tar that sprayed over him with every strike. The creature bent under the blows, whimpering and crying out until, after minutes of relentless beating had passed, it lay still and broken at the Coalman's feet.

He picked up the creature and carried it over to the cart through the assorted tableaux of people that populated the street. The creature lay atop the coal and could hardly be seen. The Coalman unhitched the cart from his petrified pony. He pulled the cart and its cargo away from the village.

The Coalman dug a shallow grave in the centre of Black Meadow and laid the foul creature to rest there. He returned to the village to resume his duties, hoping to find his pony awake, alive and with ears flicking. Alas, when he arrived, everything was as he had left it. The Priest was waving, the Milkmaid was still smiling and the children were still coming in from play; all of them frozen, all of them still, all of them statues of flesh. The Coalman, though worried, resolved that this would pass as it had before and finished delivering his coal, laughing through his worry at how surprised the villagers would be at the suddenness of their coal delivery.

But as the hours passed and his travails were completed he saw that all was still, all was frozen. He ran from door to door, opening each and running inside but found all occupants stiff and still, stuck at their rudimentary tasks. He became desperate, shouting himself hoarse at the village and in the faces of his silent customers. But as loud as he shouted, they did not respond. Their faces were unmoving, frozen in rictus grins, frowns and grimaces.

He walked to the Milkmaid and put his face next to hers, he tried to stare her down, tried to make her blink. He was sweating from exhaustion. He put his hand to his head and it came away covered in black sticky ooze; *Coal-dust and perspiration* he thought, *coal-dust and perspiration.* He looked into the face of the smiling Milkmaid, wishing that she was looking at him and not at the Priest. He moved around in an attempt to get her still eyes to lock with his, but even when he stood in front of the Priest he could tell that she was looking right through him.

He brought up his blackened hand to touch her face and as he did he noticed with excitement that her face did change. It changed in colour. He felt hope that she would come to life and that smile would be for him. But her face turned from fleshy pink, to pale, to blue, to grey. Her eyes yellowed, but she did not move or change position. She did not smile at him.

He turned and walked away towards the well, suffering a desire, an overwhelming thirst for water. He wanted to wash off the blackness and get the taste of black oil from his mouth. The bucket was in the hands of the innkeeper and try as he might he could not prise it from his stone-like grip. But the thirst, the need to be clean overwhelmed him. He climbed over the side and dropped down into the water with a grateful splash.

He drank and drank but could not lose the taste or the sensation on his skin. After some time he climbed back out again and found that the air had turned cold. He was relieved by the change and saw that the sky had turned snow grey. He looked about. The tableaux were familiar. There were the children playing in the snow, the boy floating in mid-fall and the red-haired girl with a snowball about to strike her button nose.

He ran towards her, looking around for the creature. He could save her, if he could take her from here. He stood before her and brought his black oil-dripping hand up to her face. As he touched her he was filled with hope that she would be fine, that she would not suffer. But her skin turned from fleshy pink, to pale, to blue, to grey.

Her eyes yellowed.

He looked about and saw movement. At last this stillness was over. But no, everything else remained frozen. He saw the Coalman staring at him in horror and then he knew. He saw it all. He turned and ran back to the well.

He stayed down in the water for many hours crying black tears down his oil face. When the sky changed colour, he climbed to the surface where he gratefully received a fatal beating from a kindly Coalman.

He looked up from where he lay and saw at the window the
dark black head with its shining eyes glaring in.

The Black Dog

An unhappy man lived alone in a small house on the edge of the Black Meadow. His wife had died some years previously and they had never had any children. He worked for the local Squire; building walls and mending fences, but he found the work tiring and unrewarding. The Squire did not know who he was, had never learnt his name and never gave him a word of thanks. The pay was so low that he struggled to survive from week to week. And his wife; how he missed his beautiful wife. At times he would be comforted by the thought of her but then, in an instant, the knowledge that she was gone would come flooding back. He worried and fretted and panicked and brooded, more and more, worse and worse, as each day passed. His work would occupy his thoughts in the day but when he paused for a sip of water or a hunk of cheese, it would all coming flooding in, drowning him in darkness, panic and despair.

One evening, as he finished hammering in a final post, he heard a growling near his head. He turned but could see nothing. He packed away his tools and checked that the post was solid, giving it a careful shove, before slinging his bag over his shoulder and making his way home.

He walked a path that was lined with trees on either side and as he trudged along the stony ground he could hear the padding of four paws alongside him, keeping pace. He could hear panting, a low growl. He quickened his pace, not daring to look to the side for fear of what he might see. But as he walked faster, so too did the animal in the trees. He stole a glance to his left and gasped. He caught a glimpse of sleek black fur shining in the dusk, muscles rippling beneath, as it strode alongside. The beast must have stood at least five-foot from paw to spine. With a sob of fear he broke into a run and cried out as the creature increased its speed. There was a flurry of movement. With an eruption of snapped twigs, flurries of dead leaves and clouds of dust, it exploded onto the path.

The man sprinted for home without looking back. The black dog snapped at his heels. He reached the door and sensed the creature only a few feet behind him. Key in hand, he unlocked the door and ran inside, slamming it swiftly.

The dog began to bark. The horrendous sound was pitch enough to cause goose pimples. In every bark he could hear the snap of jaw, the drip of drool and the primeval anger of a creature determined to bite. He locked the door and ran to the centre of his meagre dwelling, pulled the kitchen table towards the door and pushed it up against it.

The ferocity of the dog's call increased. It must have heard the scrape of the table against the floor. The man sank down to the ground, weeping. As he wept, the barking grew louder and more intense.

After some time the man rose to his feet. The black dog at the door had not relented in its vocal attack and was now scratching at the wood. The man screamed for the dog to leave him be, but the dog howled louder in response. The man hammered at the door, begging and screaming for the hound to go, but it did not diminish its noise. He had a few heavy pots and pans in the kitchen. Terrified, he took them to the window. After flinging it open he launched the largest pan at the black dog's head, striking it with a vicious blow. The black dog yelped and snarled and turned its attention to the window. Swiftly the man threw his stewing pot at the dog's head, following it with his frying pan and a copper kettle. The dog whimpered, drew back. It turned and fled into the meadow. He watched it retreat into the distance. Once he was certain it was out of sight, he pulled the table from the door, ran outside and retrieved his precious pots and pans.

He put the room back in order and, still shaking from his ordeal, boiled himself some plain soup with a few old potatoes and one solitary swede.

As he sat down at his table sipping at the soup, facing the chair formerly occupied by his wife, he heard the panting at the door. He froze; his spoon at his lips. The scratching began again, insistent, urgent, violent. It stopped. He heard the dog padding away. He breathed a sigh of relief and swallowed his soup. Suddenly an almighty crash shook the house; it was followed by a yelp. The sound of padding paws retreated into the distance. After a few seconds, the crash came again. There was a pause and soon after another bang at the door.

The barking began anew. Howl followed howl, ferocious, insistent, terrifying, then a crash. The man slid off his seat and sunk to the floor. He crawled to the window and peered out. By the light of the moon he could see the black dog padding away from the house, with something of a limp, before it ran with great speed at the door.

The man made for the pots. He opened the window and launched them one after another in weary panic at the desperate hound. The dog did not relent. Its howling continued. It repeatedly crashed against his front door.

"It will not stop," thought the man. "It will not cease."

So he pushed the table against the door once more and resolved to ignore the beast. He lay down upon his mattress in the cold room, shutting his eyes against the bangs and barks. But try as he might he could not sleep. At one moment the barking stopped and the man opened his eyes, hoping that the black dog had finally relented. He looked up from where he lay and saw at the window the dark black head with its shining eyes glaring in. As the dog saw him it barked again. It ran at the door, smashing and crashing against it, barking and howling and yelping with pain at each incessant blow. On and on through the night; over and over and over, never stopping, never silent, never ending. The man tried to put a pillow over his head to drown out the terror. He put his fingers in his ears and sang loudly the lullaby his mother had sent him to sleep with so many years ago, but none of these things brought comfort or an end to the relentless noise.

Hour after hour passed and eventually the light of dawn began to creep through the window. The man lay there, wide awake, whilst the dog bashed and banged and barked and howled.

"Enough!" screamed the man. "Enough!"

He ran to the log pile and pulled out his wood axe. He walked to the table, pulled it back to the centre of the room and stood by the shuddering door, mad with fury, fatigue and fear.

He waited for a bang before unlocking the door. Certain that the dog was beginning a new run at the house, he opened up. The dog flew into the room, smashing onto the stone floor. Righting itself, it turned to face the man, eyes flashing. The man shut the door, holding the wood axe, waving it in the dog's face.

The black dog and the man stood still. The hound panted, its tongue lolling, blood dripping from its bruised hide and head. The man faced it, his heart racing. The sound of his own pulse was pounding in his head, louder than the low growl coming from the throat of the black dog.

With brutal swiftness, the dog ran at the man. He swung up his axe ready to strike and the dog stopped in its tracks looking up at him. It began to howl. It was a howl so long, that the man's arm grew heavy and tired. He lowered his axe. It was a howl so mournful, that the man felt tears spring to his eyes. His own sob escaped and joined the call of the hound in an unhappy unison. It was a howl so full of fatigue that the man sank down to the floor and wept and wept and wept.

The black dog stopped its howl and padded over to the man. It licked the tears from his face and nuzzled at his hand. The man continued to weep but felt a lightness, a change and a powerful urge to sleep. He walked over to the bed and the dog followed him. It curled up next to the man as he lay on the mattress, allowing the man to go to sleep with his hand resting on its head.

He slept for a day and a night with the black dog by his side. And in the morning of the following day he embraced the hound tightly, opened the door and watched it with a smile as it padded away into the mists of the Black Meadow.

Tales from the Black Meadow
Double CD

This Exclusive Tales from the Black Meadow Double CD contains:

Disc 1 - 20 music tracks (Each one linked to a story from this book)

Disc 2 - Radio 4 Documentary: "**The Curse of the Black Meadow**"
Plus Additional Tales

4 Page Booklet including a sleeve note from Novelist and Comic book writer Warren Ellis.

Includes immediate download of 10-track album in your choice of high-quality MP3, FLAC, or just about any other format you could possibly desire.

To purchase please visit -
thesoullessparty.bandcamp.com
It is also available for download from itunes and Amazon